Farmer Brown Shears His Sheep

a Yarn About Wool

by TERI SLOAT   illustrated by NADINE BERNARD WESTCOTT

SCHOLASTIC INC.

New York Toronto London Auckland Sydney
Mexico City New Delhi Hong Kong

For my husband, Bob,
who can spin a good yarn —T. S.
For Sarah —N. B.W.

ISBN 0-439-28835-5

Text copyright © 2000 by Teri Sloat.
Illustrations copyright © 2000 by Nadine Bernard Westcott.
All rights reserved. Published by Scholastic Inc., 555 Broadway, New York, NY 10012, by arrangement with Dorling Kindersley Publishing, Inc. SCHOLASTIC and associated logos are trademarks and/or registered trademarks of Scholastic Inc.

12 11 10 9 8 7 6 5 4 3 2 1   1 2 3 4 5 6/0

Printed in the U.S.A.   08

First Scholastic printing, September 2001

Book design by Sylvia Frezzolini Severance
The illustrations for this book were painted in watercolor.
The text of this book is set in 16-point Stempel Schneidler.

Farmer Brown was shearing sheep,
  Piling up a snowy heap
    Of wool that filled his shed, knee-deep.

Clip-clip, buzz-buzz,
He took their wool and left them fuzz.

He filled his bags up, one by one,
With fleece, but when his work was done,
Clouds had covered up the sun.
The sheep saw all their wool in sacks—
"BAAA!" they cried. "We want it back!"

Soon the farmer's sheep were shivering.
They followed him—he was delivering
All their wool to Mr. Greene,

Who washed it out

And combed it clean.

Comb-pull, comb-pull,
He cleaned and carded all their wool.

Their fleece made such a fluffy stack!
"BAAA!" they cried. "We want it back!"

The sheep went running, cold and shaking,
Behind the farmer—he was taking
All their wool to Mr. Peale,

Who owned the finest spinning wheel.
Twist-hum, twist-hum,
What had their fluffy fleece become?

From fleece to yarn, it stretched and changed—
"BAAA!" they cried. "Our wool looks strange!"

Chilly sheep, with goose bumps, crying,
Rode right behind the farmer, flying
Down the road to Mrs. Muller,

Who changed the yarn from white to color!
Dip-dye, drip-dry,
The yarn grew bright before their eyes.

And while it dried upon the rack,
One sheep cried, "BAAA! Let's take it back!"

"What's this?" the farmer asked his sheep.
"You're tangled up from head to feet!
You're shivering cold and turning blue!"

So back to Farmer Brown's they flew.

He found his favorite place to sit.
Then Farmer Brown began to knit.

Knit-purl, knit-purl,
The farmer's fingers looped and twirled.

Crowded on the porch together,
Trembling in the nippy weather,
They watched him knit . . .
And when he quit,

He put a sweater on to fit
Each sheep, and then he buttoned it!

The sheep grew nice and warm again,
In brightly colored cardigans,
In patterns made of red and green
And all the colors in between.

Now each year, come shearing time,
The sheep wait eagerly in line
To feel the clip and hear the buzz,

And wear bright sweaters over fuzz.